Dear Parent:

Congratulations! Your child is taking the first steps on an exciting journey. The destination? Independent reading!

STEP INTO READING® will help your child get there. The program offers five steps to reading success. Each step includes fun stories and colorful art. There are also Step into Reading Sticker Books, Step into Reading Math Readers, Step into Reading Write-In Readers, Step into Reading Phonics Readers, and Step into Reading Phonics First Steps! Boxed Sets—a complete literacy program with something for every child.

Learning to Read, Step by Step!

Ready to Read   Preschool–Kindergarten
• big type and easy words • rhyme and rhythm • picture clues
For children who know the alphabet and are eager to begin reading.

Reading with Help   Preschool–Grade 1
• basic vocabulary • short sentences • simple stories
For children who recognize familiar words and sound out new words with help.

Reading on Your Own   Grades 1–3
• engaging characters • easy-to-follow plots • popular topics
For children who are ready to read on their own.

Reading Paragraphs   Grades 2–3
• challenging vocabulary • short paragraphs • exciting stories
For newly independent readers who read simple sentences with confidence.

Ready for Chapters   Grades 2–4
• chapters • longer paragraphs • full-color art
For children who want to take the plunge into chapter books but still like colorful pictures.

STEP INTO READING® is designed to give every child a successful reading experience. The grade levels are only guides. Children can progress through the steps at their own speed, developing confidence in their reading, no matter what their grade.

Remember, a lifetime love of reading starts with a single step!

Thomas the Tank Engine & Friends

A BRITT ALLCROFT COMPANY PRODUCTION

Based on The Railway Series by The Reverend W Awdry

www.stepintoreading.com
www.thomasthetankengine.com

Educators and librarians, for a variety of teaching tools, visit us at
www.randomhouse.com/teachers

Library of Congress Cataloging-in-Publication Data
James goes buzz, buzz / illustrated by Richard Courtney. — 1st ed.
p. cm. — (Step into reading; Step 2)
"Based on The railway series by the Rev. W. Awdry"
SUMMARY: James, a red train engine, tries to get rid of a group of bees that are plaguing him.
ISBN 0-375-82860-5 (trade) — ISBN 0-375-92860-X (lib. bdg.)
[1. Railroads—Trains—Fiction. 2. Bees—Fiction.] I. Courtney, Richard, 1955– ill. II. Awdry, W.
III. Series: Step into reading. Step 2 book.
PZ7.J1556 2004   [E]—dc22   2003020090

Printed in the United States of America
First Edition 10 9 8 7 6 5 4 3

James Goes Buzz, Buzz

Based on *The Railway Series*
by the Rev. W. Awdry

Illustrated by Richard Courtney

Random House 🏠 New York

It was a sunny day.

Chirp! Chirp!

sang the birds.

Buzz! Buzz!

hummed the bees.

Trevor the Tractor Engine
was hard at work.

Chug! Chug!
James pulled up.
"Hello, Trevor,"
said James.
"You look as busy
as a bee."

"I am!" said Trevor.

Buzz! Buzz!

"What is that noise?"

asked James.

"Bees," said Trevor.

"I am taking this beehive
to the station."

Buzz! Buzz!

b___ d the bees.

"Bees are very loud!"
said James.
"Do not make them mad,"
said Trevor.
"They may sting you!"

"Hmmmph!" said James.
"I am not scared of
a bunch of bees!"
James puffed off.

The next day,
James chugged into
the station.
He saw boxes
and bundles
and bags.
And there was
the beehive!

People rushed
this way and that.
BUMP!
A porter bumped
into the beehive!

The beehive broke!

Buzz! Buzz!

The bees buzzed

around the station.

Buzz! Buzz!
The bees buzzed
around James.
"Buzz buzz off!"
said James.
The bees
did not listen.

The bees buzzed onto
James' hot boiler.
One of the bees
burned his foot.
Buzz! Buzz! Buzz!
The bee was angry.

He stung James
on the nose!

"Eeeeeeeeeek,"
tooted James.
"Bad bee!"
James tried to make
the bees buzz off.

20

Chug! Chug!
James chugged
out of the station.

Whoosh!
He spun around
on the turntable.
Buzz! Buzz!
The bees liked the breeze.

Splash!

He tried to wash

them off.

Buzz! Buzz!

The bees took a bath.

Puff! Puff!

James blew smoke

at the bees.

Buzz! Buzz!

The bees did not budge.

James had an idea.
He turned around.
He chugged back
to find Trevor.

Buzz! Buzz!

The bees were home.

They buzzed back

into a beehive.

"Good bees!" said James.

"Goodbye, bees!"